About this book

Lucy and Tom Cat
are off to the beach,
where this amazing
adventure begins...

LUCY

TOM CAT

If you get stuck, there are answers on pages 31-32.

On the beach

Lucy sat down to read her book. It was all about dragons and monsters. Nearby, Tom Cat was hungrily watching fish when, suddenly, he let out a yowl.

Lucy looked up quickly, but couldn't see what was wrong.

Look at the opposite page. Can you see anything strange in the water?

4

Lucy meets Horace

To Lucy's astonishment, she turned around to see a huge, green sea monster rearing up out of the waves.

Lucy felt scared – but then the sea monster started talking.

"I'm Horace," he said in a gentle voice.

"I'm Lucy," she replied, "and this is To..." But Tom Cat had vanished!

Can you spot Tom Cat?

The adventure begins

"I must rescue Tom Cat!" cried Lucy.
"I'll help you," said Horace. "Hop on!"
Lucy clambered on and held on tight.
They whooshed through the water. Lucy
spotted several silvery shapes swimming
alongside them. Dolphins!

"Have you seen my cat?"
Lucy called out.
"Try Blue Bird Island," squeaked one,
nudging a map to Lucy with its nose.

Which one do you think is Blue Bird Island?

Blue Bird Island

Horace swam quickly to Blue Bird Island. Lucy jumped ashore and ran up the beach.

"I don't suppose you've seen a cat?" she asked some children tying up their boat.

The island has a tower on it . . .

"Not here, I'm afraid," said one boy. "Have you tried One Tree Island? I think cats like it there."

Can you find One Tree Island?

. . . with a pointed turret, like a witch's hat . . .

. . . and no other buildings.

11

Finn the fishergirl

Horace zipped across to One Tree Island. They met a fishergirl named Finn and asked her about Tom Cat.

"I think I know where he is," she said, thinking hard.

"Really?" asked Lucy hopefully.

"Yes, but it's a dangerous voyage to get there. You'll have to weave through spiky coral, jagged rocks and lurking sharks.

"Then, you have to go to Shell Isle and find twelve yellow shells shaped like starfish. Give them to old Toby and he'll show you the way to the Lost Lagoon. Oh, and one last thing, can you help me find *my* friend, Sid the squid?"

Can you find Sid?
How many other squids can you see?

The coral maze

Lucy and Horace arrived at the spiky coral maze.

"Oh dear," said Horace. "It won't be easy to get through. The coral is razor sharp and there are other nasty things too. Gulp!"

The white flag marks the way out. Can you find the way, steering clear of coral and creatures?

15

Shell Isle

"Phew, I'm glad that's over," said Horace as they reached Shell Isle.

Lucy gasped with delight. There were pretty shiny shells everywhere and everything was made of shells too! She began to collect some in her basket.

Then Lucy remembered that she had special shells to find.

She dashed around and found all twelve yellow star-shaped shells. Now they just had to find old Toby.

Can you spot the twelve yellow star shells that Lucy needs?

17

The Lost Lagoon

Lucy stopped in surprise
when she saw old Toby.
He was a merman!

Toby smiled down
at her and swished
his scaly tail. He
carefully counted
the shells.

"You may enter the
lagoon!" he declared.
Horace swam in, past
bright tutti frutti trees
and tropical birds.

On dry land, they were just wondering what to do next, when a face popped out of the leaves.

"Yoo hoo, I'm Olivia," she called. "I'll help you find your cat if you help me spot the Golden Spotted Wonderbird. Its tail has five gold spotted feathers that curl up."

Can you spot the Wonderbird?

The Rainbow River

When Olivia saw the Wonderbird
she jumped for joy.

"Thank you! Your cat went along
the Rainbow River," she pointed.

"Gosh, it looks a bit
choppy," said Lucy.

Horace tried to swim, but
they swirled and whirled
and splashed and spluttered.

They tumbled through a waterfall and bobbed up to the surface, gasping. Lucy looked around and caught sight of something very familiar.

What has Lucy spotted?

Under the Sea

Tom Cat was caught in a whirlpool.

"Don't worry," said Horace, "help is here!"

Lucy gawped as a small fish popped up.
It began gulping air and growing bigger
and bigger and bigger.

"It's a puffer fish," Horace told her.

The fish blew a giant air bubble around Lucy and she floated underwater. From inside, Lucy watched the wonderful, watery world. At the bottom, a strange fish began talking in bubbles, but the words were all jumbled up.

What is the fish's message?

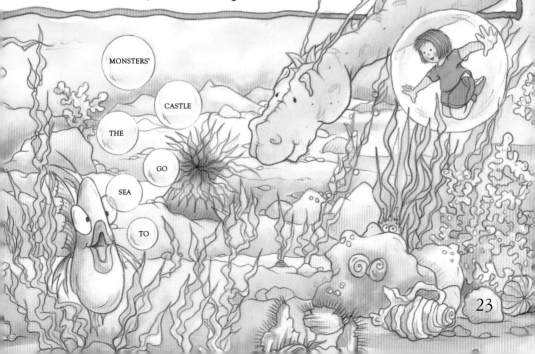

MONSTERS'

CASTLE

THE

GO

SEA

TO

23

The galleon

Lucy watched shimmering fish, and playful turtles chasing each other. As the reeds rippled apart, she looked into the black mouth of a dark cave.

Horace disappeared inside and Lucy followed. At the end of the tunnel was a sunken galleon, half-buried in the sand. But Lucy couldn't see Horace anywhere.

Where is Horace? Can you find him?

Horace's home

"Hold on tight," said Horace. Lucy grabbed on to his tail and floated along until they reached a fairytale castle.

"This is my home," said Horace proudly. "The sea monsters with two wobbly antennae on their heads are my family. The rest of the sea creatures are my great friends. Welcome!"

How many sea monsters do you think there are?

27

Surprise party

Lucy's bubble popped and she wandered into the castle. It was magical! Horace introduced her to all sorts of weird and wonderful sea creatures.

They went into a huge hall where a
delicious feast was laid out.

"We're having a party to celebrate
your visit," said Nessie, Horace's sister.
"Our other special guest is already here."

Who is the other special guest?

29

Goodbye

Lucy gave Tom Cat
a great big hug.
The party started
and everyone ate and sang
and danced for hours.

Then it was time to go. Lucy and Tom
Cat climbed onto Horace's back and
thanked their new friends.

Almost before they knew it, they were
back at the beach where their adventure
had begun.

"I'll be back soon," Horace promised as
Lucy and Tom Cat waved goodbye.

Answers

Pages 4-5

A green sea monster is coming closer to Lucy's rock. It is circled in the picture.

Pages 6-7

Tom Cat is being washed out to sea.

Pages 8-9

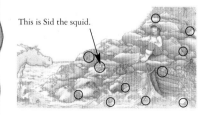

Lucy decides that this must be Blue Bird Island. It is the only one with blue birds on it.

Pages 10-11

This is One Tree Island. It has only one tree, a tower with a pointed turret and there are no other buildings on it.

Pages 12-13

There are eleven little squids including Sid. You can see them all circled here in the picture.

This is Sid the squid.

Pages 14-15

Lucy's and Horace's way through the coral maze to the open sea is marked in black.

Pages 16-17

You can see the twelve yellow star-shaped shells that Lucy has to find circled here.

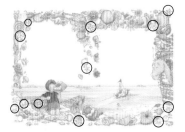

Pages 18-19

This is the Golden Spotted Wonderbird. Can you see his five curly tail feathers?

Pages 20-21

Lucy has spotted Tom Cat. Here he is.

Pages 22-23

When you put all the words in the right order, the fish's message is, "GO TO THE SEA MONSTERS' CASTLE."

Pages 24-25

Here is Horace. He is well hidden behind the plants.

Pages 26-27

You can see the ten sea monsters marked here.

Pages 28-29

Did you spot the other special guest? It is Tom Cat.

This edition first published in 2007 by Usborne Publishing Ltd., Usborne House, 83-85 Saffron Hill, London EC1N 8RT, England. www.usborne.com Copyright © 2007, 2002, 1995 Usborne Publishing Ltd. The name Usborne and the devices 🦁 🎈 are Trade Marks of Usborne Publishing Ltd. All rights reserved.